This book belongs to:

_____

Disney
Tuck-in Tales

Stories of Friendship

Disney
Tuck-in Tales

Stories of Friendship

SCHOLASTIC INC.

New York   Toronto   London   Auckland   Sydney
Mexico City   New Delhi   Hong Kong   Buenos Aires

Published by Scholastic Inc.,

90 Old Sherman Turnpike, Danbury, Connecticut 06816.

ISBN 0-7172-6913-2

Printed in the U.S.A.

First printing, May 2004

Designed by North Woods Design Group

CONTENTS

FISH SCHOOL

Written by Seymour Mackerel

Illustrated by Philip Hom, Hom & Hom Illustration and John Loter

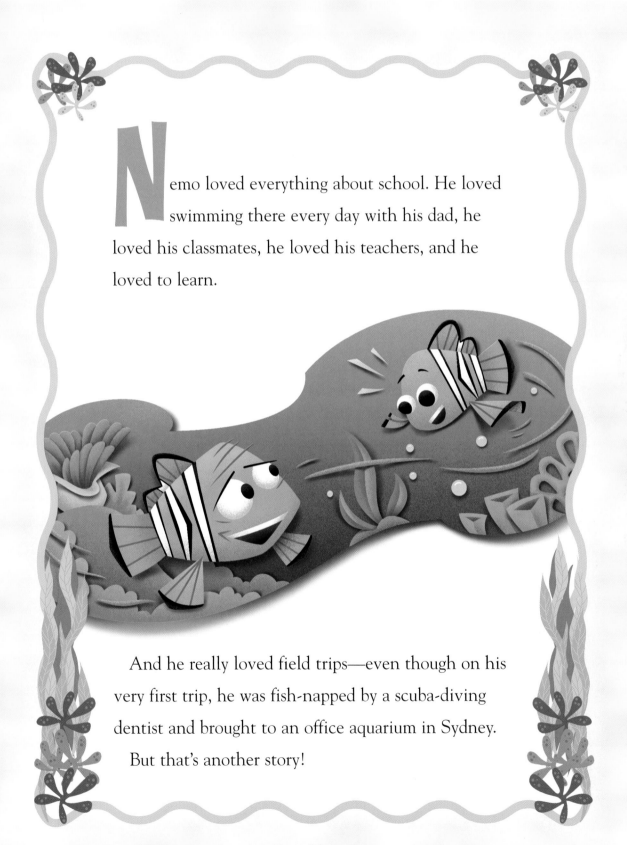

Nemo loved everything about school. He loved swimming there every day with his dad, he loved his classmates, he loved his teachers, and he loved to learn.

And he really loved field trips—even though on his very first trip, he was fish-napped by a scuba-diving dentist and brought to an office aquarium in Sydney. But that's another story!

Every morning, Nemo's dad, Marlin, would take him to school. Along the way, Nemo always liked to ask his dad lots of questions.

"What is a whale's tongue like, Dad?" Nemo asked.

"Well, it's kind of big and—" Marlin began.

"How many clownfish can a shark eat in one gulp?" Nemo wondered.

"Well, I guess it depends on the size of the—" Marlin started.

"Actually, why are we called clownfish?" Nemo asked. "You're not funny at all!"

Nemo saw his best friends, Tad, Pearl, and
Sheldon. They loved to play tag and "algae in the
middle" before school started.

Mr. Ray was on schoolyard duty that morning. He was everyone's favorite teacher. Nemo and his friends had a special song they made up just for him.

"He's our favorite teacher.
Hip, hip, hooray
For the big, spotted manta.
We love Mr. Ray!"

Then it was time for school to begin. The first class of the day was music, taught by Señor Seaweed. Nemo and his classmates were getting ready for the spring concert. Nemo played the conch shell. Sheldon played the clams. (The clams didn't like it very much!) Tad strummed along on some kelp. And Pearl played sand-dollar tambourines!

Mr. Ray taught science. Today's lesson was "Your Ocean Home."

Mr. Ray called on Nemo. "Where do you live?" he asked.

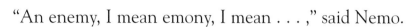

"An enemy, I mean emony, I mean . . . ," said Nemo.

"Nemo lives in an anemone," said Mr. Ray. "While the rest of us would be hurt by an anemone's stings, Nemo brushes himself against the anemone every day, so the stings don't bother him."

The rest of the class looked at Nemo in awe.

"That's right!" Nemo said proudly.

Then it was lunchtime!

There were a lot of lunchroom rules: no inking in the lunch area; no throwing worms; and no eating your classmates, no matter how tasty they look.

Nemo took out his lunch. "I'll trade you my kelp sandwich for your algae pizza," he said to Tad.

"Yum!" said Tad.

After lunch was recess. Yay! Everyone had fun playing hide-and-seek, but then Sandy Plankton got into a bit of trouble.

"It's like my dad always says," said Nemo. "It's all fun and games until someone gets stuck in a giant clam."

Once Sandy was free, it was time for Nemo's next class. It turned out that there was a guest teacher that day—Dory!

"Hi, Elmo!" she cried, waving to Nemo.

Dory was teaching the class how to speak whale.

"Repeat after me," she instructed. "*Eeyouurbawlla kaava. Pwonk! Pwonk! Froooomaafkapleweyoo.*"

"What did you say?" the class asked eagerly.

"I just said hello!" Dory exclaimed.

Then it was show-and-tell time. Pearl brought in a cool piece of coral she had found. And Sheldon, the sea horse, had some big news—his dad was having babies!

"Who wants to go next?" asked Mr. Hermit.

Nemo raised his fin. "Today I have some very special visitors for you all to meet. Come right in, guys."

Anchor, Bruce, and Chum swam in. "Pleased to meetcha," said Chum. "Don't worry, kids. We don't eat fish anymore. Well, we try not to anyway."

After a brief question-and-answer period, the sharks left. Everyone breathed a huge sigh of relief.

All too soon, it was time to go home. The students filed into the schoolyard to wait for their parents to pick them up.

Nemo couldn't wait to see his dad and tell him about all the fun things that had happened.

They sang the rest of the Mr. Ray song as they waited:

"He's our science teacher.

We think he is swell.

Sometimes we act goofy,

but he never does yell."

"Aw, shucks," said Mr. Ray, looking pleased.

Soon Nemo's dad arrived. "How was your day today, son?" he asked Nemo, as they swam home.

"Oh, Dad, it was awesome!" Nemo cried. "Sandy got stuck in a clam, Dory taught whale, and I brought in the sharks for show-and-tell. . . ." He paused to take a breath. "I can't wait till tomorrow!"

Marlin shook his head sadly. "I'm sorry, Nemo. I can't let you go to school tomorrow . . . because . . .

. . . tomorrow's Saturday!"

Mowgli Finds His Place

Written by Victoria Saxon

Illustrated by Alvin S. White Studio

owgli stretched slowly in the warm sunlight. He had slept well among the roots of a huge old tree. The day before, he had run away from the Man-village.

"Woo-hooo!" he cried, leaping up from his bed of leaves. It sure felt great to be back in the jungle!

Suddenly Mowgli stopped in his tracks. Stretching down from the tree was the sneaky snake Kaa.

"You mussst be very sssleepy," Kaa said, his eyeballs whirling. Mowgli slipped quickly under Kaa's spell.

Just then Bagheera the panther crept down from a boulder. "Leave the boy alone!" Bagheera commanded. Startled, the snake lost his balance and fell to the ground. When he landed, he found his tail tied in a knot!

As Kaa creaked away, Bagheera turned back toward Mowgli and licked his face.

"What?" Mowgli mumbled. "What happened?"

"You were hypnotized by that snake Kaa," Bagheera explained.

"Bagheera!" Mowgli said. "Boy, am I glad to see you!"

"I'm glad to see you, too, my boy!" Bagheera replied. "But what are you doing back in the jungle?"

"I decided to come home," Mowgli announced.

"But whatever for?" Bagheera asked. "You belong in the Man-village. That's your home now."

"No, it's not!" Mowgli replied bitterly. "I don't fit in with them. I don't know any of their silly games. I don't like the taste of their food. And I can't understand their language. I just don't belong, Bagheera. Please let me come home," he pleaded. "Take me to Rama and my wolf family."

"Very well," Bagheera replied. "I'll take you back for a short visit, but that's all. Now hop up on my back."

Mowgli and his wise old teacher began the journey toward the home of his wolf family. "He'll find his place in the Man-village sooner or later," Bagheera told himself, as he padded through the jungle.

"Bagheera," Mowgli said after a while, "I've been thinking. Maybe you could teach me to be a panther. Then I could stay with you in the jungle where I belong."

"You are a Man-cub, Mowgli," Bagheera said. "I can't—"

"Please?" Mowgli begged. "I'll do everything you tell me. We could at least try, couldn't we?"

"Very well," Bagheera said at last. "We'll try. Now hop down. I want you to climb that tree over there."

Mowgli jumped off and tried to climb up the tree. But his hands slipped. Bagheera had to give him a boost.

"Here, like this," said Bagheera. Mowgli watched as his friend dug his claws into the tree and climbed its trunk. Bagheera climbed past Mowgli and leapt to the next branch.

"I'll show him," Mowgli thought with great determination. But when Mowgli tried to jump from one branch to another, he slipped and tumbled onto the soft soil below the tree.

"I'll never be a panther!" Mowgli said angrily. He grabbed a fistful of dirt and threw it on the ground. "I don't have claws, and my legs aren't strong enough!"

Bagheera sighed. "Don't worry, Mowgli," he said. "We're almost at Rama's den. You'll have a nice visit with him. Then you can return to the Man-village."

"Or," Mowgli said, "I can learn to be a wolf!"

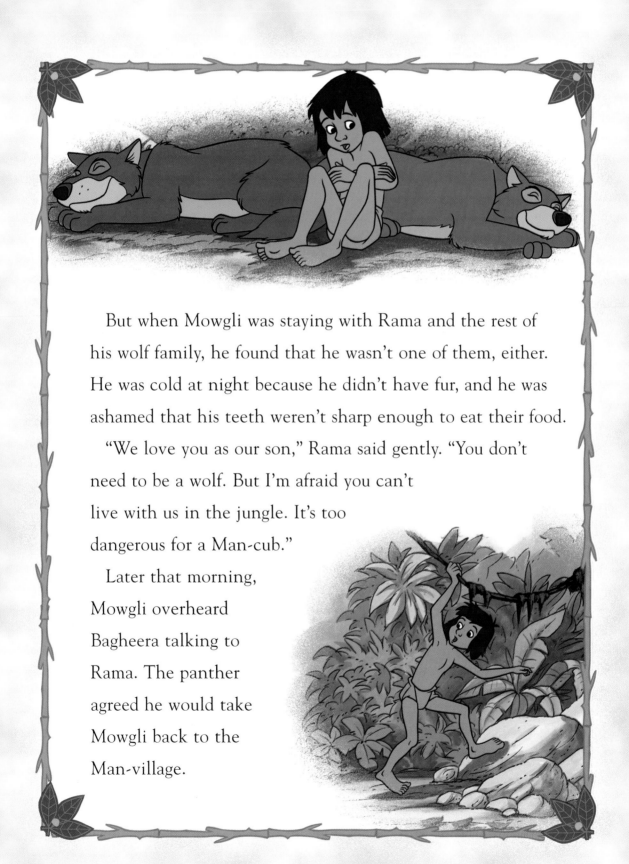

But when Mowgli was staying with Rama and the rest of his wolf family, he found that he wasn't one of them, either. He was cold at night because he didn't have fur, and he was ashamed that his teeth weren't sharp enough to eat their food.

"We love you as our son," Rama said gently. "You don't need to be a wolf. But I'm afraid you can't live with us in the jungle. It's too dangerous for a Man-cub."

Later that morning, Mowgli overheard Bagheera talking to Rama. The panther agreed he would take Mowgli back to the Man-village.

Mowgli just knew he'd be miserable and unhappy in the Man-village. So he sneaked away into the jungle when no one was looking. He ran until he came to a stream, where he flopped down on the mossy bank and started to cry.

"Why all the tears, buddy?" a voice interrupted him.

"Because I don't belong anywhere!" Mowgli wailed.

"Well, I think you look fine right where you are," the voice said gently.

Mowgli looked up then and saw a great big, happy-looking bear sitting next to him. "Baloo!" Mowgli cried happily. "Where did you come from?"

"Well, when I heard you were back in the jungle, I had to come and welcome you, Little Britches."

"Baloo," Mowgli asked, "would you teach me to be a bear, so I can live here with you?"

"Aw, kid, why would you want to live like a bear?"

"Because I don't feel like I belong anywhere!" Mowgli complained.

"I don't understand the ways of the Man-village, and I'm not a good panther or wolf. I don't have claws or sharp teeth or fur or strong legs!"

"Slow down, kid," Baloo said. "I've got an idea."

Baloo led Mowgli toward a grove of banana trees. As they walked along, they sang happily.

Suddenly Baloo stopped. "Hey, kid," he said, "I'll race you to that banana tree!"

"You're on!" Mowgli cried. Then he raced ahead of his friend and easily won the race.

"Good job, Little Britches," Baloo said. "Now, can
you give me a hand reaching some of those bananas?
I'll lift you up, and you grab a bunch."

"Sure, Baloo," Mowgli said. He scrambled up on Baloo's
shoulders and plucked several bananas. Then
the two friends settled down for lunch.
After lunch, they went for a walk.

"Well, Mowgli, what do you
think?" Baloo finally asked.
"Do you really still think
you don't fit in
anywhere?"

Mowgli
thought
quietly for
a moment.

"I'll tell you what I think," Baloo said. "I think your long legs help you run fast, and your hands may not have claws, but they're sure good at picking fruit. Your teeth are fine for chewing bananas. And you're about as much fun to be with as anybody I know. See, kid? You're perfect just the way you are."

Mowgli smiled.

"I guess I could learn

to talk to the other Man-cubs.

They would probably teach me their games,

too. And maybe I can teach them about my jungle

friends. Then maybe I would fit in with them better."

"I bet you could," Baloo said.

Early the next morning, Baloo walked with Mowgli to

the edge of the Man-village.

"Baloo," Mowgli said, as he turned to say good-bye, "can I still come back and visit you?"

"You can go wherever you want, kid," Baloo replied. "Now go show 'em what ya got!"

And with that, Mowgli headed to the village. He knew he could fit in just fine.

Good Morning, Sleepyhead

Written by Amy Bauman

Illustrated by Alvin S. White Studio

Winnie the Pooh awoke feeling a little . . . a little . . . well, a little as if he didn't know how he felt. He sat up in bed and looked out the window. It wasn't raining, but it was a gray and gloomy day.

"This isn't at all the kind of day I had hoped it would be," he said to himself.

Pooh sighed. It was bad enough feeling the way he felt. But it was even worse not knowing exactly what it was that he was feeling. Pooh sat very still, trying to decide what the strange feeling was. But no matter how hard he thought, he just couldn't figure it out.

Finally, Pooh pulled himself from his snuggly bed.

"If anyone would know how a bear is feeling on such a gray day, Piglet would," he said to himself. So, tucking a jar of honey under his arm for the trip, Pooh went off to Piglet's house.

Piglet was home when Pooh arrived. Piglet was in the kitchen opening drawers and peeking under things.

"Good morning, Piglet," called Pooh, hoping Piglet would invite him in.

"Good morning, Pooh," Piglet answered. But he continued his search. He was so busy, he didn't seem to realize that Pooh was there.

"Are you looking for something?" Pooh asked finally, having watched Piglet for some time.

"Yes," Piglet answered. "I keep a list of ways to cheer myself up on a gloomy day. And today being that kind of day, I thought I'd check my list."

"Oh," Pooh said. "And what does your list say?"

"I don't know!" Piglet squealed. "I can't find it!"

It was plain to see that Piglet had a problem of his own this morning. Pooh could also see that Piglet's problem was making him just a little grumbly.

Problems didn't make Piglet grumbly except on gloomy days.

So Pooh walked on, feeling a little . . . well, the same as he'd been feeling before.

Pooh hadn't gone far when he came upon Tigger. Tigger was sitting in the middle of the path, stretching and scrunching his tail. First he'd stretch it as far as it would stretch. Then he'd scrunch it as tightly as he could.

"Hello, Tigger," Pooh said.

Tigger looked up. "Oh, hello, Pooh. I'm having a little bounce trouble today."

"That's too bad," Pooh answered. "Say, Tigger—"

"A tigger's bounce is a wonderful thing, you know," Tigger went on.

"It is," Pooh agreed. "Tigger, would you know—"

"Without his bounce, a tigger is nothing," Tigger whispered to Pooh.

Pooh sighed. The cloudy day had even taken the spring out of Tigger's tail. It was clear to Pooh that Tigger wouldn't be any help, either.

Rabbit's house was just down the road. Pooh could see Rabbit standing in his garden. As Pooh came closer, he could hear Rabbit grumbling about what a gray day it was.

"My vegetables really need some sun!" Rabbit was harrumphing. He stomped back and forth in his garden as he grumbled. "We haven't had a decent sunny day in weeks!" Rabbit, who often sounded cross, sounded a little more cross than usual.

Pooh decided it wasn't the right day to ask Rabbit if he knew how a bear might be feeling.

At the end of the path, Pooh came to Owl's house. Owl was home, too, but he was fast asleep. It wasn't like Owl to sleep all day, but he was tucked down tight and looked as if he meant to stay that way.

Pooh found a comfortable spot to rest while he waited for Owl to wake up. After a while, waiting made Pooh hungry, so he pulled out his honey jar to give himself a treat. On such a gloomy day, Pooh thought, a treat might be a good idea.

The honey *was* a good idea, but it didn't make the feeling go away, and Owl wasn't waking up. "This gray day has gotten to everyone," Pooh said to himself. "Everyone is just too busy or too out of sorts to help me figure out how a bear might feel on such a day."

45

Now feeling disappointed on top of everything else, Pooh decided to head home. So he turned and made his way back along the route he'd come—past Rabbit's house, past the spot in the road where Tigger was still working on his tail, past Piglet's house, and back finally to his own little home.

"On such a gray day, it might have been better if I had just stayed in bed," Pooh said to himself. He thought a moment. "Or maybe I'll go back to bed!" And with his honey jar in his arms, he did just that.

But no sooner had he climbed back into bed and snuggled down beneath his covers than Piglet, Rabbit, Tigger, and Owl appeared at the door!

"Well, hello, everyone!" Pooh called. His friends

46

trooped in and stood around the bed.

"We just came by to see how you are, Pooh," Tigger said, and everyone nodded.

"You did?" said Pooh.

"Yes," returned Rabbit. "I'm afraid that I was making such a fuss about my garden earlier that I didn't even think to ask what you needed."

"And I was so busy looking for my list that I didn't even realize you were there," added Piglet.

"So what DID you need, Pooh?" Owl asked.

"Well," Pooh began, fumbling with the covers, "it was a cloudy day when I woke, and I was feeling a little . . ."

"Grumpy?" Rabbit suggested.

"Grumbly?" asked Piglet.

"Growly?" Tigger said.

"No . . . not grumpy, not grumbly, and not growly," Pooh answered thoughtfully. "I was feeling a little . . ."

"Sad," a voice cut in. Everyone turned to see who had said it. Standing in the doorway was Eeyore. He'd come by looking for everyone else.

"On such a gloomy day, I often feel a little sad," Eeyore admitted, "as if I could use a hug."

"That's it EXACTLY!" Pooh shouted, jumping out of bed.

"Well, why didn't you say so?" Tigger laughed. With a new spring to him, he bounced Pooh, Eeyore, Piglet, Rabbit, and Owl into one huge heap of hugs.

The friends stayed that way until all the sadness had been squished out of everyone. At last, they pulled apart and sat down for a bit of tea and honey with Pooh.

"On such a gray and gloomy day, everyone needs a hug," Pooh said with a smile.

"A bear hug," Piglet offered.

"Yes, Piglet, a bear hug." Pooh sighed—happy now. It was great to have such good friends. Maybe the day hadn't ended up to be so gray and gloomy, after all.

MICKEY THE DRAGON SLAYER?

Written by Liane Onish
Illustrated by Alvin S. White Studio

ickey Mouse whistled as he rode. It was a fine, windy day for a traveling organ player and music teacher.

Around the bend, the wind grew even stronger. Mickey held onto his hat. Leaves, twigs, and straw swirled around his wagon.

As he drove by an open field, Mickey saw Goofy trying to fly a kite in the strong wind. "Hello!" Mickey cheerfully called. Goofy, struggling to keep his feet on the ground, was too busy to answer. Parents and disappointed children were hurrying away with their kites at their sides. "Golly!

It's even too windy to fly a kite," Mickey said to himself, still holding on to his hat.

Mickey drove past a pond. "Wak!" Donald squawked angrily. "Wak! Wak!" Mickey saw that Donald was struggling to gather up the toy boats on his pond—before the wind broke them. He was trying to return the sailboats to their owners so they could get them safely home.

The wind blew and blew. As Mickey got closer to town, a poster blew off a pole right into his face. Mickey didn't have a chance to read what the poster said: "Wanted: Hero to Slay Windy Dragon."

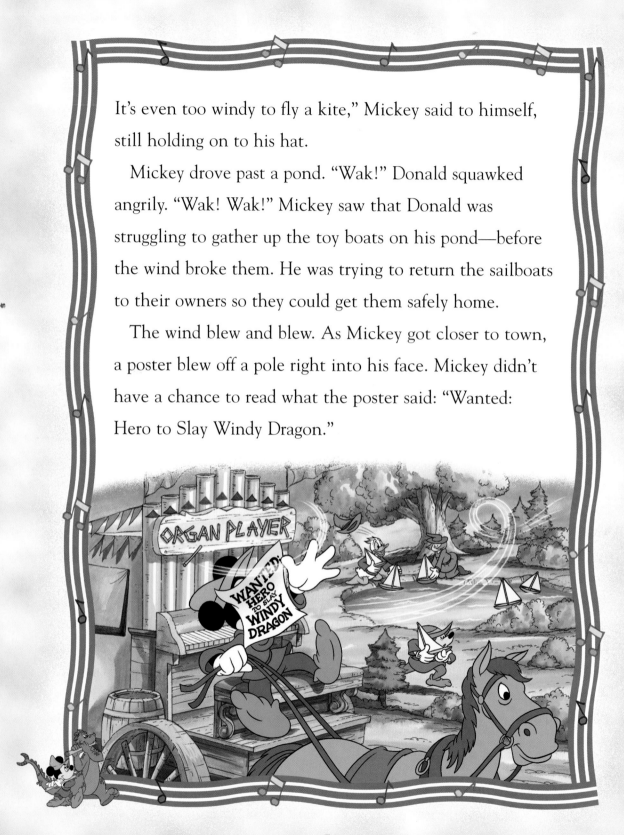

Just then the Mayor rushed up. "At last you're here!" he cried.

Mickey was surprised. "What a warm welcome for a traveling—"

The Mayor interrupted. "You're just what we need, Mister Dragon Slayer! But before you go to work, you'll want a fine meal. Come along to Miss Minnie's."

"Dragon slayer?" Mickey gulped. "What does he mean?"

As the Mayor climbed up to drive the wagon, Mickey read the poster that he had peeled off his face. But before he could explain that there had been a mistake, the Mayor said, "Here we are! Miss Minnie will take real good care of you." And the Mayor rushed away.

"But . . . ," Mickey began. Then he saw Miss Minnie and he couldn't say another word. Mickey was in love.

Miss Minnie said shyly, "Welcome, Mickey. We're so glad you've come to slay the dragon."

"But I'm not a dragon slayer," Mickey told her. He pointed to the sign on his wagon. Then Mickey saw the trick the wind had played with his sign. A twig had blown onto the letter O, and the letter P had broken. Now the words were not quite the same. *Organ Player* had become *Drgan Slayer!* Uh-oh!

Goofy and Donald rushed up to Mickey and Miss Minnie. "Gawrsh," said Goofy, "it's a real honor to meet an honest-to-goodness dragon slayer! If you slay that Windy Dragon, *Goofy's Ye Olde Go Fly a Kite* business will really take off!"

"Hmmmph," snorted Donald. "You don't look like a dragon slayer to me. But if you are, it will be smooth sailing for *Donald's Ye Olde Go Float a Sailboat*."

"Good luck, Mister Dragon Slayer! The whole town is counting on you!" Goofy called, as he and Donald left.

What could Mickey do? He followed Miss Minnie into her Bake Shoppe, hoping to think of something—anything.

But even Miss Minnie's most delicious muffins didn't give him any ideas. Not knowing what else to do, Mickey got onto his wagon and drove out of town into the wind. The whole town cheered and waved him on his way. Mickey put on a brave smile and waved back. Only Miss Minnie knew the sad truth. But she waved and blew him a kiss. Mickey hoped she would understand when he came back without having slain the dragon—*if* he came back.

Mickey drove into the wind toward the hills. It was slow going. Then suddenly the wind stopped. Mickey stopped, too. "What happened to the wind?" he wondered. "I don't see anything. I don't hear anything. And I don't know what to do next!" So Mickey did what he always did when he didn't know what to do. He took out his flute, sat down, and began to play.

After playing several tunes, Mickey sensed he wasn't alone. Still playing, he slowly turned around. Standing there was a not very large, but definitely very curious, dragon.

"Oh!" said Mickey. "You must be the Windy Dragon."

The dragon nodded and sighed sadly. The force of his sigh knocked Mickey over.

"Wow! It must be hard to make friends if you blow them over!" Mickey said.

The dragon nodded again and helped Mickey up.

"Oh, that's okay," Mickey said. He felt sorry for the dragon. "I wish there was something I could do to help."

The dragon pointed to the flute, and he gestured for Mickey to play.

Mickey played a sad tune and saw a tear roll down the dragon's cheek. "Bet you're awfully lonely," Mickey said.

"When I feel lonely, I play music. It cheers me up."

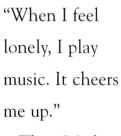

Then Mickey had an idea. "Maybe I could teach you to play music! Would you like that?"

The dragon nodded. Mickey gave him the flute and showed him how to blow into it. Smash! The force of the dragon's breath shattered the small instrument. The dragon looked even sadder.

"Hmm," said Mickey, thinking. "I know!" He took an extra organ pipe out of the wagon and carved some dragon-sized finger holes in it. "Here we are—a dragon-strong flute!"

Mickey was a good music teacher, as well as an organ player. In a few hours, the dragon had learned to control his breath and play his special dragon-strong flute. By evening, the dragon and Mickey—who also had a new flute—were playing duets. They sounded great!

Mickey drove back to town with the dragon hiding inside his wagon. He arrived in the town square to cheers and welcomes from everyone.

Mickey held up his hands, and the crowd quieted down.

"There's someone I'd like you all to meet," he said. Mickey opened the curtain, and out stepped the dragon. The townspeople drew back in horror. "This is the Windy Dragon," Mickey said. "He and I would like to play for you." Together, Mickey and Windy played and played.

"Hey, they're really good!" said the banker.

"Cool!" said the iceman, dancing with the greengrocer.

Then Mickey explained that Windy had learned to control his windy breath by playing music.

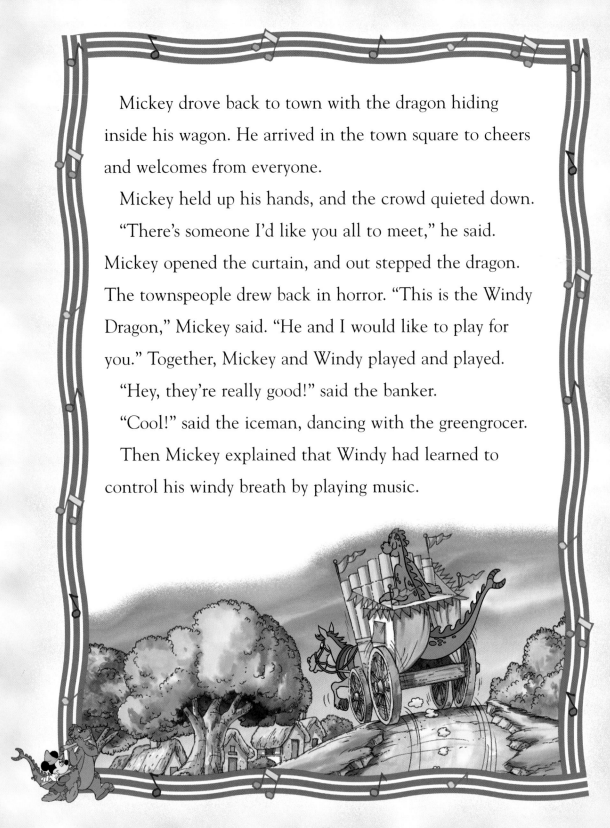

"Gawrsh, does that mean Windy could make a nice steady breeze to fly kites?" asked Goofy. "If he can, he's got a job at *Goofy's Ye Olde Go Fly a Kite!*"

Windy nodded yes, and he and Goofy shook hands.

"Hmm, could Windy make a gentle breeze to sail toy boats?" asked Donald. "If he can, he can work for me at *Donald's Ye Olde Go Float a Sailboat* pond."

Windy nodded yes again and shook Donald's hand.

Miss Minnie added, "Windy, if you have some time, could you come by the Bake Shoppe on baking day and stoke the oven?" Windy nodded yes again and again. Miss Minnie hugged the dragon. Then she hugged and kissed Mickey, and the crowd cheered.

The Mayor said, "Mickey, we had no idea you were a dragon slayer and a music teacher!"

Mickey laughed. Then he pulled the stuck twig out of the O on the sign on his wagon and fixed the broken P. "To tell the truth," he said, "I never was a dragon slayer—just a traveling organ player and music teacher."

"I'm so glad," said the Mayor, who was also the schoolteacher. "I was afraid you were just a bad speller!"

65

Walt Disney's
Peter Pan

Tink Gets Her Jingle Back

Written by Amy Bauman

Illustrated by Alvin S. White Studio

Not long after Wendy, John, and Michael Darling returned from Never Land, Peter Pan appeared at their nursery window one evening. Everyone was asleep, but Wendy—ever watchful for Peter—heard his whispered call.

"We need your help, Wendy," Peter said. Only then did Wendy see Tinker Bell's bright glow; she hadn't heard the pixie's familiar bell-like voice.

"Tink's lost her voice," Peter explained, "and she insisted you were the only one who could help her."

"Of course I'll help," Wendy answered, waking her brothers. She turned to Tinker Bell in time to see her give a great big sneeze. "Oh dear! Tinker Bell must have caught a cold! Hmm."

Tink crossed her arms over her chest and glared at Wendy, blinking rapidly.

"Tink says only humans 'lose' their voices because of colds," Peter translated. "She says her voice is *really* lost. We have to find it and reattach it—just the way you did with my shadow."

"Find her voice? Reattach it?" Wendy exclaimed. "Goodness! I think she'd be better off drinking hot tea and getting some sleep. But if she thinks searching will help, that's what we'll do. Where shall we start?"

Tinker Bell zoomed across the room again, blinking more rapidly than before. This time she was excited.

"Slow down, Tink!" Peter sighed. Even without her jingling bell, he was able to understand his winged friend, but it was hard when she blinked so fast.

"She says her voice is out there somewhere," Peter said, pointing to the darkened city of London.

Wendy sighed. "It's a big city," she said. "Let's get started."

With a happy twirl, Tinker Bell sprinkled pixie dust over everyone, and they rose into the air alongside Peter. One by one, they flew out of the window to soar high above the city streets.

"Did you hear that?" Wendy shouted suddenly, when they'd flown some distance from the Darling home. She circled in the air, and everyone pulled up beside her to listen. Sure enough, a delicate jingling sound arose from the park below.

"That sounds about right," Peter said, cocking his head to one side to hear the sound better.

Tinker Bell nodded and excitedly led the group down, where they found . . . a cat!

"That's certainly not Tinker Bell's voice," Michael exclaimed. "It's the bell from that cat's collar."

The tabby glanced up at the group and then dashed into the bushes. They could hear the frantic *jingle, jingle* of its collar long after the cat was out of sight.

"Well, that was just our first try," Wendy said cheerfully. "Let's keep looking."

With a whoosh, everyone rolled skyward. They were soon even farther from the children's quiet little street and their warm beds. It was then that they heard a second bell tinkling.

"Down there!" Peter called. He zipped down through the clouds. John, Wendy, and Michael—and Tinker Bell—were on his heels when they discovered that this "voice" was a . . . carriage bell!

"Git up, there," the carriage driver called to his horse. He made a clucking noise and tugged on the reins. The bell jingled as the old horse clip-clopped off.

"That's not Tink's voice, either," Peter said, sitting down on a cloud. As Wendy, John, and Michael gathered around him, Tinker Bell fluttered slowly up to the group, looking tired. She sneezed three times—silently, of course—and rubbed her eyes.

"Oh, Peter," Wendy whispered. "I'm certain Tinker Bell has a cold, and that's how she lost her voice. Can't you make her rest?"

Peter laughed. "You can't make Tink do anything she doesn't want to do," he said.

"Then we'll have to go on looking to keep her spirits up until her voice returns," Wendy decided. She jumped into the air. "Come on, everyone! We've got a long way to go tonight."

Tinker Bell was the first to lift into the air. She gave Wendy a shy smile and then zoomed ahead, her bright light leading the way. The group wound its way across the night sky behind her, flying up one street, down another, across this meadow, and back over that forest. Even as morning approached, they kept on following each bell they heard, sure that it would be the right one.

One bell, they discovered, belonged to a cow named Doris. It hung from a rope tied at her neck and clanked as the old girl moved about. Up close, it didn't even sound right.

Another bell turned out to be the bell over a bakery door.

It jangled each time someone went in or out—although, at this hour, when most people were still sleeping, it wasn't ringing a lot.

"The wind must have made it ring," said Michael.

They found a church bell, a bicycle bell, a bell attached to a garden gate, and even an old ship's bell that rang as the boat rocked gently in the river. But none was Tinker Bell's voice.

The pixie's wings drooped as they discovered yet another bell that wasn't hers. By now the rising sun was sending its rays over the horizon. Soon she and Peter would have to leave.

"Don't give up hope, Tinker Bell," Wendy said. She held out her hand, and to her surprise, the pixie landed on her finger.

"You can come back tonight, and we'll search again."

"Yes," John added. "We'll keep looking until we find your voice, no matter how long it takes."

"Of course we will," Wendy said, as they turned for home. "Wait! There's one more bell to check. But it's kind of far away. Tinker Bell, why don't you curl up in my pocket where it's quiet and warm until we get there?"

To everyone's surprise, Tink did as Wendy suggested. Once inside the pocket, the fairy fell asleep almost immediately.

"Well, look at that!" Peter whispered. He turned to Wendy. "We'd better hurry, Wendy. Tink and I don't have much time left."

Wendy led them back. They flew across the meadow, over the river, back into the heart of London, and right up onto the face of the biggest clock in the city. The big clock hands

ticked to the hour just as they arrived. Its huge bell began ringing.

Just then Tinker Bell awoke from her nap. With a yawn, she climbed to the edge of Wendy's pocket and launched into the air. Her light blinked madly as she flew round the clock.

"What's she saying?" Wendy shouted over the clock's noise.

Peter chuckled with Tinker Bell, who was looping through the air, rolling with laughter. "She's wondering how you could have thought this huge bell could be her voice."

The clock hit its last note, then fell silent.

"That's funny," John said. "The clock stopped, but my ears are still ringing."

"Mine, too!" Michael laughed.

Wendy shook her head. "That ringing isn't your ears! It's Tinker Bell! She has her voice back!"

It was true. Tinker Bell's high, sweet voice rang out clearly. Still jingling, she landed on Wendy's shoulder.

"Tink wants to know if you really thought this bell was hers," Peter told Wendy.

Wendy smiled at Tinker Bell. "No. I knew this bell was much too big to be your voice. I also knew that, with a little time and sleep, your voice would be fine. I'm sorry to have tricked you."

Tinker Bell smiled, jingling, and kissed Wendy's cheek.

Then she yawned.

"Tink doesn't mind, Wendy," Peter answered, yawning, too.

John couldn't help himself, and he yawned, too. Little
Michael rubbed his eyes and hugged his bear tightly.

"We really must get home, Peter," Wendy said, "and you
and Tinker Bell must hurry back to Never Land."

With that, Peter, Tink, Wendy, John, and Michael rose one final time into the air and headed home to their warm beds and sweet dreams.

A Little Help From a Friend

Written by Victoria Saxon

Illustrated by Alvin S. White Studio

"**Y**ippie!" Kiara exclaimed. "C'mon, Daddy, wake up! You promised we could walk the Pride Lands together. Today's a perfect day!"

Kiara's father, Simba, stretched and gave a great big yawn. Kiara shuddered. Her father's yawn always sounded like a roar to her. Someday she, too, would have a big roar like her father's. Then all the animals in the Pride Lands would respect her. She would be able to go wherever she wanted whenever she wanted.

When Kiara and Simba stepped outside, Timon and Pumbaa were waiting for them.

Kiara sighed. She knew why they were there. When would
everybody stop treating her like a baby?

Just then Zazu flew up to Simba. "Sire!" Zazu exclaimed.
"Some Outsiders have been spotted in the Pride Lands—near
the western canyon. You'd better come at once."

Simba turned to Kiara. "I'm sorry," he said. "Our walk will
have to wait."

"That's okay," Kiara answered. "I'll just hang out around
here. I won't go too far. I promise."

But Simba knew his daughter's adventurous spirit all too
well. "Just stay in sight of Pride Rock at all times. And take
Timon and Pumbaa with you wherever you go."

"Aw, Daddy," Kiara complained.

"Kiara, I don't have time to discuss this," Simba said.

Kiara watched her father head off on another adventure. Why couldn't she go with him? She could help him chase all those mean Outsiders back to their home in the Outlands.

Then Kiara had an idea. She thought she could remember how to get to the western canyon by herself. All she would have to do was lose Timon and Pumbaa somewhere along the way. That should be easy enough. She'd certainly done it plenty of times before.

"Wait for us!" Timon and Pumbaa shouted as they scrambled after her. Soon the trio was crossing a wide, grassy plain.

"Hey, Timon," Pumbaa said as he looked at a grove of trees. "Isn't that where we found all those juicy grubs last week?"

"Pumbaa, Pumbaa, Pumbaa," Timon said, "which one of us knows where to find grubs?"

"Well, you do, Timon, but—"

"So let me tell you about those trees over there, Pumbaa," Timon said. "Those trees—hey! That's where we found all those grubs last week. Pumbaa, I'm a genius!"

Timon hopped onto Pumbaa's back. "To the grubs, Pumbaa!"

Then Timon turned to Kiara. "Follow us, Princess. You're about to experience a feast fit for the future queen!"

Kiara followed them—but only because she knew this would be her best chance to escape.

Sure enough, as soon as Timon and Pumbaa found their grubs, they completely forgot about Kiara. The lion cub quickly slipped away through the trees, giggling to herself.

Suddenly Kiara heard a growl. Then a ball of fur tackled her, rolling her over and over. When Kiara caught her breath, she was looking into the eyes of a male lion cub not much bigger than she was. He was trying to look very ferocious, but he had mud on his nose. And his growl sounded feeble. Kiara couldn't help it. She had to giggle.

"What are you laughing at, Pride Lander?" the other cub snarled.

"Well . . . ," Kiara hesitated, "actually, I was laughing at you." Then she burst out in another round of uncontrollable giggles.

The other cub sneered grumpily. Then he looked more closely at Kiara. He had met her once before. She was the one who had taught him to play tag!

"Kiara?" the cub asked. "Hey! It's me—Kovu!"

"Kovu?" Kiara said. "Cool! I was wondering if I'd ever see you again!"

"Hey, want to play tag?" Kovu asked.

"Oh, my gosh!" Kiara interrupted. "I can't play. I was on my way to find my dad. He went to chase some Outsiders away from the western canyon. Want to come along?"

"Nah," said Kovu, "I'll just stay here by myself."

"Why?" asked Kiara. "It'll be totally cool. They'll go, 'Roar!' and then my dad'll go, 'ROARRRRRR!' Then those Outsiders are going to turn into a bunch of scaredy cats, and my dad'll chase them away!"

"Kiara, I'm an Outsider. Remember?"

"Yeah, but—but you're not like the other Outsiders, Kovu. You're fun," Kiara replied.

"Aw, forget it," Kovu said. "Go on. I don't need to play with you anyway. I have plenty of things to do here by myself."

Kiara started to leave. Then she stopped. It really would be more fun to stay and play with Kovu.

Kiara raced back to Kovu and tapped him on the back. "You're it!" she cried, as she raced away.

Kovu gave chase. "I'll get you!" he cried.

Suddenly both cubs came to a halt. "What was that noise?" asked Kovu.

"It sounds like. . . ." Kiara hesitated. Then she knew what the sound was. It was Pumbaa! And he was in trouble.

Kiara and Kovu ran toward the sound of Pumbaa's voice. They found him pacing around at the base of a tree, looking up helplessly.

"Pumbaa, what's wrong?" Kiara asked.

Pumbaa explained. Timon had climbed the tree to find some good bugs but had lost his balance. He'd hit his head on a branch and knocked himself out. Luckily, his foot had become tangled in a vine. Timon hadn't fallen, but now his foot was slipping out of the vine loop.

Kiara knew she had to help. This would take some fast thinking. Hmm . . .

Suddenly she had an idea!

Kiara turned to Kovu and asked him to climb the tree. Then she jumped on top of Pumbaa's back. Now she was just inches away from Timon. When Kovu had climbed high enough, Kiara asked him to chew right through the vine holding Timon's foot. When Timon fell, he landed safely on Kiara's back. But he still wasn't very alert.

"C'mon, Kovu," Kiara urged, as she headed back to Pride Rock with her two baby-sitters. "We need to get Timon home."

"I don't think I'd better come with you," Kovu replied. "Outsiders aren't welcome in the Pride Lands."

Kiara looked back at her friend. "I guess you're right," she sighed. "See you later, then."

"Hey, Kiara!" Kovu called to her. "You were really great. That was some quick thinking you did."

"Thanks." Kiara smiled. "You did some quick climbing."

On the way back to Pride Rock, Timon began to feel better. Pumbaa told him all about how Kiara and the Outsider had saved him.

"Gee, Kiara," Timon said, "maybe next time you should be *our* baby-sitter."

Kiara beamed with pride.

"But let's agree not to tell Simba about the Outsider, okay?" Timon added. "Let's just say he was a friend."

When the trio reached Pride Rock, Simba was waiting for them. The warning about the Outsiders had been a false alarm.

When he heard what had happened, Simba turned to his daughter. "You must have thought quickly to save Timon," he said. "I'm very proud of you."

Kiara looked at Pumbaa and smiled. Then she thought of Kovu. "It was nothing, Dad. It just shows what you can do with a little help from your friends."